THE ADVENTUR[...]

THE BAILEY SCHOOL KIDS®

VAMPIRES DON'T WEAR POLKA DOTS

WITHDRAWN

A GRAPHIC NOVEL BY PEARL LOW

BASED ON THE NOVEL BY
MARCIA THORNTON JONES & DEBBIE DADEY

Gift from:

graphix

An Imprint of

SCHOLAS[...]

FOR MY MOM AND BEST FRIEND, THELMA THORNTON
— MARCIA THORNTON JONES

FOR ALEX — DEBBIE DADEY

I DEDICATE THIS BOOK TO THE IMAGINATION WITHIN
ALL OF US; IMAGINATION THAT ALLOWS US TO SEE THE
WORLD WITH CURIOSITY, WONDER, AND AWE — PEARL LOW

Library of Congress Control Number: 2020941106

ISBN 978-1-338-73660-1 (hardcover)
ISBN 978-1-338-73659-5 (paperback)

10 9 8 7 6 5 4 3 2 1   21 22 23 24 25

Printed in China   62
First edition, August 2021

Edited by Jonah Newman
Book design by Steve Ponzo
Color flatting by Wes Dzioba
Creative Director: Phil Falco
Publisher: David Saylor

THE KIDS AT BAILEY SCHOOL

EDDIE

MELODY

HOWIE

LIZA

CAREY

BEN

CHAPTER 1 A NEW TEACHER

I *AM* SERIOUS, HOWIE! MY COUSIN GOT A WRESTLER FOR A TEACHER, AND HIS MUSCLES WERE THE SIZE OF *BEACH BALLS!*

DON'T WORRY, I CAN HANDLE ANY TEACHER — EVEN A WRESTLER.

EDDIE, IF YOU HADN'T BEEN SO MEAN TO MRS. DEEDEE, SHE WOULDN'T HAVE QUIT.

WE WERE *ALL* MEAN TO HER!

5

. . . MRS. JEEPERS.

THANK YOU, PRINCIPAL DAVIS.

IT IS WONDERFUL TO MEET YOU ALL.

I AM SURE WE ARE GOING TO HAVE A GREAT YEAR TOGETHER.

HER ACCENT IS MYSTERIOUS.

Mrs. Jeepers

I COME FROM THE COUNTRY OF ROMANIA.

JEEPERS DOESN'T SOUND ROMANIAN TO ME.

I CHOSE A NEW NAME FOR MY LIFE HERE.

I WAS RAISED IN MY FAMILY'S CASTLE IN THE MOUNTAINS OF TRANSYLVANIA. IT WAS A WONDERFUL LIFE UNTIL . . .

AT RECESS . . .

I THINK SHE'S STRANGE. HAVE YOU NOTICED HER ODD LITTLE SMILE?

I THINK SHE SMILES BECAUSE SHE'S NICE!

AND HER ACCENT IS REALLY NEAT!

SHE SOUNDS LIKE A *VAMPIRE*, LIZA. I WONDER WHERE SHE GOT THAT HUGE GREEN BROOCH?

SHE WAS RAISED IN A CASTLE. MAYBE THAT BROOCH IS AN ANCIENT WIZARD'S STONE.

CHAPTER 2 SUSPICIONS

AFTER SCHOOL . . .

BRRING!

SEE YOU TOMORROW, MELODY!

SEE YA LATER, CAREY!

HEY, LOOK!

WOULD YOU LIKE TO COME IN AND SEE?

ER...UM...
I HAVE TO GO
HOME AND DO MY
HOMEWORK.

THE NEXT MORNING . . .

MRS. JEEPERS ISN'T HERE YET . . .

CLICK!

GOOD MORNING, CLASS. I AM SORRY TO BE LATE. BUT I DID NOT GET MUCH SLEEP LAST NIGHT.

OH, NO YOU DON'T!

DON'T YOU *DARE* PULL MY HAIR, EDDIE. IT'S RUDE TO PULL PIGTAILS!

I'M SORRY, MELODY . . . I-I WAS JUST JOKING!

OK, BUT I'M NOT. YOU DO *NOT* HAVE PERMISSION TO TOUCH MY HAIR.

THAT IS QUITE ENOUGH, EDDIE. YOU MUST NEVER PULL ANYONE'S HAIR.

CHAPTER 3 THE DARE

AT LUNCH . . .

I THINK WE HAVE TO WATCH OUT FOR MRS. JEEPERS.

WHAT ARE YOU TALKING ABOUT, MELODY? MRS. JEEPERS IS A WIMP!

THEN HOW COME YOU ACTED SO FRIGHTENED OF HER TODAY?

NO TEACHER CAN SCARE ME, HOWIE!

EDDIE, YOU WERE TERRIFIED IN CLASS TODAY.

I AM *NOT* SCARED OF MRS. JEEPERS!

THEN WHY DON'T YOU PROVE IT?

SNEAK INTO HER BASEMENT AND FIND OUT WHAT'S IN THAT COFFIN. THEN WE'LL KNOW YOU'RE NOT AFRAID.

UNLESS YOU'RE CHICKEN.

I AM NOT! I'LL DO IT, HOWIE!

THAT NIGHT . . .

BOO!

DO YOU REALLY THINK IT'S A COFFIN?

THERE'S ONLY ONE WAY TO FIND OUT. DO YOU WANT TO OPEN IT . . . OR SHOULD I?

LET'S DO IT TOGETHER.

THIS THING WON'T BUDGE.

MAYBE IT'S LOCKED? BUT I DON'T SEE A LATCH.

UNLESS IT'S LOCKED FROM THE INSIDE?

THAT WOULDN'T WORK UNLESS . . .

. . . UNLESS SOMEONE WAS INSIDE TO UNLOCK IT!

QUICK, BEHIND THAT BUSH!

HUFF HUFF

WHAT MADE THAT NOISE?!

I DON'T WANT TO STICK AROUND TO FIND OUT . . .

CHAPTER 4 HYPNOTIZED

THE NEXT MORNING . . .

SO, WHAT WAS IN THE BOX?

I BET EDDIE AND MELODY CHICKENED OUT.

WE DID NOT! WE SNEAKED OUT OF OUR HOUSES AND INTO HER BASEMENT!

WHEN I WAS A CHILD IN ROMANIA WE WERE TAUGHT TO BE RESPECTFUL OF OTHERS.

WE ONLY NEEDED TO BE TOLD ONCE TO KEEP THE FLOORS FREE FROM LITTER . . .

. . . OR TO KEEP OUR CLASSROOM NEAT.

THANK YOU, CLASS. NOW, ON TO OUR LESSON.

SO, I HEAR YOU'RE SCARED OF MRS. JEEPERS!

AFTER LUNCH . . .

Spelling exercises
Please fill in the blanks:
1.) Cla __ es
2.) Frida_

BEN IS RIGHT, I HAVE TO SHOW MRS. JEEPERS WHO'S BOSS!

"SHUFFLE"
"SHUFFLE"

HEH.

SHWOOOOO

POP!

THE ANSWER
IS . . . TWELVE.

THANK YOU,
EDDIE. YOU MAY
SIT DOWN.

CHAPTER 5 NO ORDINARY TEACHER

VAMPIRES DON'T LIKE GARLIC . . .

. . . SO I BROUGHT THIS.

DO YOU THINK THAT'LL WORK?

WELL, IT'S WORTH A TRY. WILL YOU GO WITH ME TOMORROW MORNING TO SPRINKLE IT AROUND THE CLASSROOM, MELODY?

I HAVE
HAD ENOUGH.

GULP

EDDIE, COME WITH ME, PLEASE.

SLAM!

WHAT DO YOU THINK SHE'LL DO TO HIM?

I DON'T KNOW . . .

. . . BUT I'M GLAD IT'S NOT ME!

CAW!

YOU GUYS WERE RIGHT. MRS. JEEPERS IS NO *ORDINARY* TEACHER.

C'MON, EDDIE. WHAT HAPPENED? IS SHE A VAMPIRE OR NOT?

ALL I KNOW IS . . .

. . . I'LL NEVER MAKE HER MAD AGAIN!

THE END

MARCIA THORNTON JONES is an award-winning author who has published 131 books for children, including the Adventures of the Bailey School Kids series, *Woodford Brave*, *Ratfink*, and *Champ*. Marcia lives with her husband, Steve, and two cats in Lexington, Kentucky, where she continues to write, mentor writers, and teach writing classes. She is the coordinator of the Carnegie Center Author Academy, an intensive one-on-one writing program for adult writers working toward publication.

DEBBIE DADEY grew up in Kentucky and now lives in a log cabin in Tennessee with her husband and a greyhound rescue. Her three adult children continue to inspire her. A former first grade teacher and school librarian, she is the author and coauthor of 179 books, including the Adventures of the Bailey School Kids series. Her newest series, Mermaid Tales, is a multicultural series from Simon and Schuster. She also coauthored *Writing for Kids: The Ultimate Guide* with Marcia Thornton Jones.

PEARL LOW is an Afro Asian artist based in Vancouver, Canada. Her works are rooted in themes of self-love, acceptance, and Chinese and Jamaican Canadian experiences. She works in comics and animation and won an Oscar in 2020 for her work on the short film *Hair Love*.